I0610274

Nathan Haskell Dole

Joseph Jefferson at Home

Nathan Haskell Dole

Joseph Jefferson at Home

ISBN/EAN: 9783337423490

Printed in Europe, USA, Canada, Australia, Japan

Cover: Foto ©Andreas Hilbeck / pixelio.de

More available books at **www.hansebooks.com**

CROW'S NEST, SHOWING FAMILY GROUP ON PIAZZA.

JOSEPH JEFFERSON
AT HOME

BY

NATHAN HASKELL DOLE

ILLUSTRATED

BOSTON
ESTES AND LAURIAT
1898

LIST OF ILLUSTRATIONS.

JOSEPH JEFFERSON AT HOME.

A PAINTER lives in the legacy of his pictures; the poet goes down to posterity in his verses; the musical composer wins immortality by his operas or symphonies, which live on in the possibilities of the printed page; but the singer and the actor, however great their contemporary fame, quickly become only a tradition. We read of the triumphs of the Siddonses and the Ristoris, of the Grisis and the Marios, and there is nothing to bring them before our imaginations, except the extravagant encomiums of their day.

The ephemeral lot of the actor.

The praise and applause which crown the efforts of the popular actor is his compensation for the temporary character of his work.

Fortunate is the actor who lives in this later generation. The gulf, so artificial and unnecessary, that in former times separated him from society, has been practically closed; the narrow and bitter prejudice which has, indeed, always existed and in all countries, against those who "show themselves for money," who pretend to be what they are not, has largely died out. Occasionally,

Fading prejudice.

some popular preacher will rail against the theatre, or bring odium on the church by refusing Christian burial to the buskined son of the Muses; but the world, as it increases in knowledge, recognises more and more openly that prejudices are ignorant and unreasoning; they are now mainly confined to bigoted sectarians. We know that the "stage-villain" may be in his private life the pattern of propriety. The actor is not only "admired, applauded, highly rewarded, loved, envied, the object of the most flattering (not to say the most impertinent) curiosity," but, what is better, he is weighed on his own merits, and if his character and behaviour be blameless, his profession is regarded as in no respect derogatory; he is everywhere received in the most exclusive circles; he is decorated with the ribbon of the legion of honour; he is granted titles and honours; he is welcomed for his own sake.

Character of actors.

It is undeniable that the standard of character among actors has been constantly rising. Whereas the glare of publicity may seem to bring out into prominence the failings of certain erratic geniuses, on the other hand, the search-light of criticism finds that many of the most popular actors and actresses of the day are without reproach, that they lead perfectly exemplary lives, and have all the virtues of humanity. Many are those whom one might select as object-lessons of this worthi-

ness; one would, perhaps, think most naturally, at the
very first, of the name of Jefferson, borne irreproachably
through five generations, and culminating in the fascinating and admirable personality of Joseph Jefferson, the
Rip Van Winkle so dear to thousands. It is with
Joseph Jefferson, the third to bear that honoured name,
that this unpretentious monograph has to deal, not so
much for the purpose of defending the stage, as to
gratify a laudable desire on the part of many to have
a compact sketch of the life, and particularly of the
home life, of an actor who has been so long before
the footlights, and secondly, to lay an humble wreath
at the feet of one whom we all are proud to honour.

I.

JOSEPH JEFFERSON was born in Philadelphia, Feb. 20, 1829, at the southwest corner of Spruce Street and Sixth Street. In his autobiography, he says that he could almost claim to have been born in a theatre; his earliest recollections were connected with one; his first play-house was, in both senses of the word, a playhouse;

Early
passion
for acting.
"behind the scenes" he could amuse himself with "those sure tokens of bad weather, the thunder-drum and rain-box," or play hide-and-seek in the "Tomb of the Capulets," or Ali Baba's robbers' cave; or behind the green bank, from which stray babies "were usually stolen, when left there by affectionate but careless mothers." Even when he was in long clothes, at a time before which his memory is a blank, he was carried on the stage to add realism to the scene. His earliest passion was for theatricals; he says that as he had a theatre stocked with scenery and properties, he could indulge his passion at small expense, especially as his stock company were volunteers, consisting of two little boys and their sister, who used to play with him on Saturdays.

12

JOSEPH JEFFERSON TELLING A STORY TO SOL SMITH RUSSELL, HIS YOUNGEST
SON STANDING IN THE CENTRE LISTENING, AND HIS LITTLE
GRANDSON SITTING ON ARM OF CHAIR.

This early passion for the stage was not merely the result of environment. Inheritance, reaching back nearly a hundred years before his birth, must be also called in to explain it. In 1746, a youth of eighteen named Thomas Jefferson, the son of a Yorkshire farmer, rode to London, mounted on a thoroughbred horse, and was by a happy accident immediately thrown into the society of David Garrick. He was a jovial young fellow, and so charming that he was admitted into Garrick's intimate friendship, and by his advice adopted the stage. His earliest recorded appearance at Drury Lane was in October, 1753. He took the management of several theatres, and was an actor of sterling merit in some sixty parts, and passed a highly successful life, dying in 1807, after sixty years of connection with the stage. His first wife came from a family connected with the Navy, and opposed to her becoming an actress, but she succeeded in overcoming her father's scruples, and went on the stage, playing with her husband at Drury Lane in 1753. One of their two sons became a clergyman, and went as a missionary to Africa; the other, Joseph, born in 1774, became an actor, and having some difficulties with his father's second wife, he came to America in 1797, for a salary of seventeen dollars a week, and the payment of his passage, offered by Charles Stuart Powell, the first manager of the Bos-

Inherited talents.

Joseph Jefferson the first.

ton Theatre. By the time that Jefferson reached Boston
Powell had failed, and the Federal Street Theatre was in
other hands.   It is possible that he played as one of the
witches in " Macbeth," in December, 1795, but his first
important appearance in this country was in February of
the following year, when he played the part of " Squire
Richard " in "The Provoked Husband."   He was described as small and slender, with a Grecian nose, blue
eyes full of laughter, and an unrivalled capacity for
exciting mirth.   He seems to have inherited his father's
love for a good joke, — a characteristic that has been
handed down, like a Toledo blade, from generation to
generation.   Joseph Jefferson found lodgings in New
York with a Mrs. Fortune, the widow of a Scotch mer-
chant.   Her house was next the John Street Theatre,
where he made his first successes.   She had two daughters; one, Euphemia, became the young comedian's wife;
the other, eleven years later, became the second wife of
William Warren, and the mother of no less than six
children, all of whom find mention in the history of
the American stage ; the fifth was William Warren,
who for over forty years was the mainstay of the
Boston Museum company, Boston's especial pride and
favourite in many varied parts.

Mr. and Mrs. Jefferson both accepted an engagement
at the Park Theatre, his service lasting five years, hers

Inherited
love of
humour.

lasting three. It is said that his greatest successes were made in the delineation of old men; and one of his favourite autobiographical anecdotes relates how a philanthropic lady once called at the Park Theatre with a subscription blank, and begged the managers to withdraw that poor old Mr. Jefferson from the stage. She had seen him as "Item," in "The Steward," and she felt that it would be only Christian charity to provide for such an aged and feeble person. She herself had headed the subscription with a generous sum, and was on her way to increase it, in order to provide a home for the infirm old man in his declining years. Thomas Cooper, a fellow actor, listened to her generous scheme, and assured her that the management would gladly coöperate in relieving Jefferson's condition. At that propitious moment Jefferson himself came in, and Cooper had the pleasure of presenting him to his benefactress, who was amazed to see such a handsome young man, and could hardly believe her eyes. She tore the subscription-blank into pieces and went away, not sadder, but wiser.

A philanthropic scheme.

In 1803, the Jeffersons moved to Philadelphia, and joined the company playing at the Chestnut Street Theatre, with which their fortunes were identified until the theatre was burned down in 1821. After Jefferson's popularity gradually declined. His wife died

The Jeffersons in Philadelphia.

in January, 1831, and he himself, disappointed and suf-
fering from the disease of gout, which he had inherited
and vainly struggled against, "closed his pure and
blameless life" in Harrisburg, eighteen months later.
William Winter sums up contemporaneous opinions of
him in the statement that "he was a man of original
mind, studious habits, fine temperament, natural dignity,
and great charm of character, and his life was free from
contention, acrimony, and reproach." He had the gift
of making people happy. The very sound of his
voice compelled laughter. "Alas! Poor Yorick!"

He appeared in upwards of two hundred characters,
but all his talents could not save him from waning popularity. Edwin Forrest spoke once with deep feeling of
"that beautiful and gifted old man; what poverty and
what purity and high morality were in his household;
how he had educated his children, and how at last he
had died among strangers, heart-broken by ingratitude."
Not wholly unappreciated! For Chief Justice Gibson

A beautiful
epitaph.
composed an epitaph for his gravestone, in which he
called him "an actor whose unrivalled powers took in
the whole range of comic character, from pathos to soul-
shaking mirth; his colouring of the part was that of
nature, — warm, pure and fresh; but of nature enriched
with the finest conceptions of genius."

He had nine children, all but two of whom adopted

JOSEPH JEFFERSON AND SOL SMITH RUSSELL AT CROW'S NEST.

the profession of acting. His second son, Joseph Jeffer-
son II., was born in 1804, in Powell Street, Philadelphia. Joseph
Jefferson
the second.
He inherited his father's talent for drawing and painting,
and he showed some proficiency in architecture. When
he was a boy of ten, he appeared at the Chestnut Street
Theatre, and played such parts as the First Murderer in
" Macbeth." Like his father, he was excellent in playing old men. In 1824 he was a member of the Chatham
Garden Theatre and met Mrs. Thomas Burke, whom he
married, though she was eight years his senior. She was
born in New York, the daughter of a French gentleman
named Thomás, who, with his wife, was on his way to San
Domingo, to take possession of an estate. M. Thomás
lived on the island until the rising of the negroes in
1804, when they were assisted to escape by a faithful
slave. He arrived penniless at Charleston, S. C., and,
through the favour of the athlete and rope-dancer, Alex-
andre Placide, then managing the Charleston Theatre, he
found humble employment behind the scenes, but not as
an actor. His now motherless daughter, Cornélie Fran- Jefferson's
mother.
çoise, first served in the ballet and afterwards in minor
parts in regular plays. She became well known as a
singer : Ireland says that she had " a pleasing face and
person, and an exquisite voice, which, in power, purity,
and sweetness, was unapproached by any contemporary." She was early married to the handsome, talented,

but dissipated Irish comedian, Thomas Burke, who died of delirium tremens in 1824, leaving one son, Charles St. Thomas, who gave great promise, but died at the early age of thirty-two. Even then he had appeared on the stage in upwards of fifty parts, and was the first to dramatise and to act the part of "Rip Van Winkle."

Joseph Jefferson III. well remembered how his half-brother spoke the line, "Are we so soon forgot when we are gone?" and, out of sweet loyalty to that lamented genius, pronounces them in a different tone. He is quoted as saying of him:

"Charles Burke was to acting what Mendelssohn was to music. He did not have to work for his effects, as I do. He was not analytical, as I am. Whatever he did came to him naturally, as grass grows or water runs. It was not talent that informed his art, but genius."

Such was the ancestry and inheritance of the future "Rip Van Winkle," an inheritance of unsullied character through five generations; of varied talents; and finally those blended strands of nationality — English, Scotch, and French — which so often result in original genius.

An unsullied inheritance.

II.

M<small>R</small>. J<small>EFFERSON</small> gives an amusing account of his first conscious public appearance, when, " in a white tunic Early appearance on the stage. beautifully striped with gold bands, and in the grasp and on the shoulders of an infuriated tragedian," he was carried across " a shaky bridge amid the deafening report of guns and pistols and in a blaze of fire and smoke. To me," he goes on to say, " the situation seemed perilous, and in order to render my position more secure, I seized 'Rolla' by the hair of his head. 'Let go,' he cried, but I was obeying the first law of nature, not ' Rolla,' so I tightened my grasp upon his tragic topknot. The battle was short but decisive, for in the next moment I had pulled off his feather-duster head-dress, wig and all, thereby unintentionally scalping the enemy ; and, as he was past the prime of life, the noble Peruvian stood bald-headed before an admiring audience."

When he was three years old, he was taken to witness a new entertainment in the shape of " Living Statues," and his imitative genius impelled him to copy the tab-leaux. He posed for his own amusement before the green-room glass as " Ajax defying the Lightning," or as

"The Dying Gladiator." His family also had the benefit of these amateur performances, and it was but a step to transfer the gifted child to the stage, to repeat them for the amusement of the public.

His aunt Elizabeth, in her recollections,[1] recalls how, when little more than two years old, he gave an imitation of Fletcher the statue man, and his grandmother, chancing to notice him in a corner of the room trying that experiment, found that he had caught all the "business" of the statues, though he could not have pronounced the name of one of them. She made him a dress similar to that worn by Fletcher, and that he made somewhat of a sensation is proved by a statement quoted from an interview with an eye-witness who recollected how little Joe, "in white fleshings, white wig, and chalked face, was placed on a small round table and gave imitations of Fletcher's statuary,—'The Discobolus,' 'Ajax Defying the Lightning,' etc. He was hardly longer than the legs of the table, but so admirably he struck the attitudes, and so perfectly proportioned was he, that the audiences were charmed with the graceful, lovely boy." He himself says:

"I am in the dark as to whether this entertainment was 'the talk of the town' or not, but I fancy not; an attenuated child representing Hercules struggling with

Jefferson and the living statues. [marginal note]

---

[1] Printed in Mr. William Winter's "Life and Art of Joseph Jefferson."

RECEPTION HALL, CROW'S NEST.

a lion could scarcely excite terror; so I presume I did
no harm if I did no good."

When he was four years old, he likewise imitated
T. D. Rice, one of the first to delineate negro characters. That fantastic "knight of the burnt cork" saw
his imitation of "Jim Crow," and insisted that the boy
should appear for his benefit. Mr. Jefferson, in his
autobiography, says: "I was duly blacked up, and
dressed as a complete miniature likeness of the original. He put me in a bag, which almost smothered
me, and carried me upon the stage on his shoulders.
No word of this proceeding had been mentioned in
the bills, so that, figuratively speaking, the public were
as much in the dark as I was. After dancing and
singing the first stanza, he began the second, the following being the two lines which introduced me:

> " ' Oh, ladies and gentlemen, I'd have you for to know
> That I've got a little darkey here, that jumps Jim Crow; '

and turning the bag upside down, he emptied me out
head first before the eyes of the astonished audience.
The picture must have been a curious one; it is as
vividly before me now as any recollection of my past
life. Rice was considerably over six feet high, I was
but four years old, and as we stood there, dressed
exactly alike, the audience roared with laughter. Rice

and I now sang alternate stanzas, and the excitement increased ; showers of pennies, sixpences, and shillings were tossed from the pit, and thrown from the galleries upon the stage. I took no notice of this, but suddenly the clear, ringing sound of a dollar caught my ear, and as the bright coin was rolling from the stage into the orchestra, I darted forward, and secured my prize. Holding it triumphantly between my finger and thumb, I grinned at the leader of the orchestra, as much as to say, 'No, you don't.' This not only brought down the house, but many half-dollars and dollars besides. At the fall of the curtain, twenty-four dollars were picked up, and given into my delighted hands." That was not the last golden, or rather silver, shower that fell at the feet of the young actor.

That performance took place in Washington. Mr. Jefferson's childhood was a kind of an Odyssey, and his wanderings were many and full of adventures. Combats were not lacking; thus at his first appearance "out of the juvenile supernumerary ranks:" He was dressed to represent a Greek pirate, and Master Titus, the son of a City Hall official, represented an American sailor. They had a fierce encounter, but young Jefferson was magnanimous, and allowed his opponent, for whose benefit the fight took place, to overcome and slay him. The fight was redemanded,

and the Greek pirate " had to come to life again, —
quite a common thing for stage pirates, — and die
twice." Mr. Jefferson recalls that he rather delighted
in being the slain foe, and having a star-spangled ban-
ner waved over him; but he is at a loss to know why
Mrs. Ireland refers to that combat as celebrated. " In
the accounts of our last war with the Greeks," he says,
" there is no mention made of this circumstance. If,
therefore, the combat was celebrated, it must have been
for historical inaccuracy."

The Jeffersons' stay in New York could not have
been very long or very successful, for though they
were there in 1835, two years later, or at the end of
the season of 1837–38, having received an invitation
from a brother-in-law, Alexander Mackenzie, to go
to Chicago and take part in the management of a new
theatre in that enterprising little town, they were in
such straitened circumstances that they had to sell certain cherished articles to procure " necessary comforts
for the trip," and in order to pay their fare on an
Erie canal-boat, they depended upon such precarious
receipts as they might get by acting at Schenectady,
Utica, or Syracuse. The captain of the canal-boat Performance on a canal boat.
had conscientious scruples against attending the theatre,
but not against taking the entrance fees. But, un-
fortunately, at Syracuse it rained in torrents, and the

attendance was light. They still owed ten dollars
passage-money. So the captain, having an inward han-
kering for the forbidden, offered to call it " square " if
the actors in the company would give him a private
show in the cabin. They declined, with a pride worthy
of the Baron de Sigognac. But Mrs. Jefferson was not
averse to show off the abilities of her son, and he was
permitted to ransom the rest. Mr. Jefferson, in his
amusing account of this episode, says:

A song for
a sail.   " The captain turned it over in his mind, — being, I
am afraid, a little suspicious of my genius, — but after
due consideration, consented. So he prepared himself
for the entertainment, the cook and my mother com-
prising the rest of the audience. The actors had wisely
retired to the upper deck, as they had been afflicted on
former occasions. I now began a dismal comic song,
called 'The Devil and Little Mike.' It consisted of
some twenty-five stanzas, each one containing two lines,
with a large margin of 'whack fol de riddle.' It was
never quite clear whether the captain enjoyed this entertainment or not; my mother said he did, for though
the religious turn of his mind would naturally suppress
any impulse to applaud, he said, even before I had half
finished, that he was quite satisfied."

Many years later, Mr. Jefferson is said to have had
another opportunity to turn an honest penny by giving

PARLOR, SHOWING CARVED FIGURES IN THE PLAY OF "RIP VAN WINKLE"
UNDER THE MANTEL.

a strictly private performance. He was out on the tranquil waters of Buzzard's Bay, when a fisherman's craft slowly drifted alongside of his boat, and the owner, seated amid the debris of his conquests, growled out:

" Be you an actor ? "

" Yes."

" Wal, here's fifty cents, and I want you should make up fifty cents' worth of faces for me."

Accordingly he flung a silver piece over into Mr. Jefferson's boat !

From Buffalo the gay emigrants, hope beckoning on, took steamer for the long and beautiful sail through the Great Lakes, a leisurely voyage, with delightful experiences of Indians and primitive life for the impressionable young Thespian. At that day Chicago contained only about two thousand inhabitants, and everything was new, even the theatre — new and crude. " Don't you think your angels are a little stiff in their attitudes ? " asked Jefferson of the scene-painter of his Chicago rival.

" No, sir, not for angels," was his reply, evidently, like the ancient bishop, mistaking angles for angels. " When I deal with mythological subjects I never put my figures in natural attitudes ; it would be inharmonious. A natural angel would be out of keeping with the rest of the work."

There may also have been a hidden sting of sarcasm in that memorable reply, reflecting on the work on the stage.

[margin note: Fifty cents' worth of faces.]

[margin note: Natural attitudes.]

III.

THEIR season in Chicago was short, and the golden prospects which the ever-hopeful hoped for in vain led them on into still newer fields. Often, says his son, when the roads were heavy and the horses were jaded, A hopeful spirit. he would see his father "trudging along ahead of the wagon, smoking his pipe and no doubt thinking of the large fortune he was going to make in the next town, now and then looking back with his light blue eyes, and giving the mother a cheerful nod which plainly said: 'I'm all right; this is splendid, nothing could be finer.' If it rained he was glad it was not snowing; if it snowed he was thankful it was not raining. This contented spirit was his only inheritance; but it was better than a fortune made in Galena or anywhere else, for nothing could rob him of it."

They travelled from Galena to Dubuque on the frozen Mississippi, but a warm spell had set in, and they could see the ice bending under the horses' feet. The passengers arrived safely, but the sleigh containing their baggage, their scenery and properties and all broke through. "My poor mother," says Mr. Jefferson, "was in tears,

34

but my father was in high spirits at his good luck, as he
called it, — because there was a sand-bar where the sleigh
went in ! "

He, poor man, had painted the scenery, and its appearance was not improved by a six hours' cold bath !   " A
wood scene had amalgamated with a Roman scene painted
on the back of it, and had so run into stains and winding
streaks that he said it looked like a large map of South
America ; and pointing out the Andes with his cane, he
humorously traced the Amazon to its source."   This
accident delayed their opening for a week, and the soaked
helmets of pasteboard were beyond repair.

What humorous memories such episodes must recall
in better, if not happier days !   Here they acted in a
court-house, there in a large warehouse ; in one place
they routed an army of pigs out of their barracks on the
prairie at the edge of the town, and, having thoroughly
cleansed and whitewashed it, they played there in " Clari,
the Maid of Milan," by John Howard Payne.   Mrs.
Jefferson sang the popular ballad of " Home, Sweet
Home," which was a part of that now-forgotten drama.
The banished pigs, who had collected under the flooring,
were so affected by the music that they set up a pathetic
wail in the midst of the song, and quite ruined it.   Mr.
Jefferson says that his mother was in tears at the unex-
pected failure ; but his father, with his usual fund of

Scenery
in the
Mississippi.

" Home,
Sweet
Home " in a
pig-house.

philosophy, consoled her by saying that, "Though the grunting was not quite in harmony with the music, it was in perfect sympathy with the sentiment."

At Springfield the two managers resolved to build a new theatre. When it was completed it was forty feet wide and ninety feet deep, looking like "a large dry-goods box with a roof." No sooner was it completed, however, than a political shyster, taking advantage of a religious revival then in progress, and working on rampant prejudices, got the town to pass a new law calling for a heavy license for "play-acting." Ruin stared them in the face. But a young lawyer came to their aid, and, by a masterly argument full of characteristic humour, completely turned the tables on the bigots. "That lawyer," says Mr. Jefferson, with pardonable pride, "was Abraham Lincoln."

Lincoln comes to their rescue.

At Memphis the Jeffersons, who had parted company with McKenzie, were stranded; and, as an ordinance had been passed requiring all carts, drays, and public vehicles to have the names of their owners painted on them, young Jefferson went boldly to the mayor and represented that his father was an artist as well as a comedian, and that, as the theatrical season was over, he was devoting his time to sign and ornamental painting. The result was that the contract was assigned to the stranded actor, and he and his son spent a month in carrying on

Art in the West.

DOWNSTAIRS LIBRARY, SHOWING A PAINTING BY JOSEPH JEFFERSON.

this artistic and lucrative avocation, while their leading man manufactured genuine Havana cigars in the same studio. He was also engaged to decorate a billiard-saloon and bar-room, and then a house, for a Scotch saloon-keeper. For this work no pay was forthcoming, and, after waiting in vain for two weeks, they took steerage passage down the river in order to reach Mobile in time for the fall season. But at the last moment Mrs. Jefferson resolved to appeal to the wife of the unjust debtor. She succeeded and returned to the boat with the hard-earned wages. This would have enabled them to travel first-class, but she persuaded her husband that it would be better to save the money and go as they had at first intended.

Misfortunes in Mobile.

This showed the contrast between the two natures of Mr. Jefferson's parents; " she was content to bear present humiliation for the sake of future good; he would willingly have parted with all his money for the sake of giving his family present comfort." So they went by steerage, and reached Mobile, to meet with worse misfortune than ever: yellow fever was raging there, and in less than a fortnight after their arrival, on the 24th of November, 1842, Joseph Jefferson II. fell a victim to the dreadful disease. Instead of going to school, young Jefferson and his sister were engaged at the theatre, to act in fancy dances and comic duets; and

employments more menial, such as grinding paints in
the paint-room, were put on the young artist. They
received, each, a salary of six dollars a week, and were
made to understand that it was given to them as a
charity.   Mr. Jefferson adds grimly to his account of
these troublous days, that if there was any charity in
the matter, it was on their side, considering the numer-
ous duties imposed on them.   Mrs. Jefferson undertook
to open a boarding-house for actors, but the season was
disastrous for " the profession," and so she found herself
in debt.   Fortunately, a benevolent lady had taken an
interest in her enterprise, and volunteered to get up a
benefit for the two talented children ; it was a success.

Jefferson
and
Macready.
At Mobile, Jefferson acted with both Macready and
the elder Booth.   He got into disgrace with Macready,
however, by accidentally setting fire to his wig.   Macready chased him all over the theatre.   The papers the
next morning declared that Macready had never in his
life acted with so much fire ; but poor Jefferson was
temporarily banished from the stage, although the fault
was clearly the actor's.

After the Mobile season was over, the company,
including the Jeffersons, went to Nashville, and travelled through the State.   On their return to Nashville, they found the river so low that steamboats
were not running ; so, although the season had been

very bad, they managed to buy a barge and fit it up, and sailed down the river " in the queerest-looking craft A journey down river. that ever carried a legitimate stock company of the old school." Jefferson declared that it was heaven; to stand his watch at night gave him a manly feeling. He helped supply the larder with wild game, and, no doubt, when they got farther down the river, and there was a fair wind blowing down stream, he took the keenest delight in their swift progress, rendered possible by unfurling a drop scene as a sail. " The wonder-stricken farmers," he says, " and their wives and children would run out of their log cabins, and, standing on the river bank, gaze with amazement at our curious craft. It was delightful to watch the steamboats as they went by. The passengers would crowd the deck and look with wonder at us. For a bit of sport, the captain and I would vary the picture, and as a boat steamed past, we would first show them the wood scene, and then suddenly swing the sail around, exhibiting the gorgeous palace. Adding to this sport, our leading man and the low comedian would sometimes get a couple of old-fashioned broadswords, and fight a melodramatic combat on the deck. There is no doubt," he adds, " that at times our barge was taken for a floating lunatic asylum."

Later the next season, he was called upon to grace

a patriotic occasion by singing the " Star Spangled Ban-
ner " at St. Louis.   His own account of his first attack
of stage fright is so delightfully humorous, that I can
not resist quoting the whole of it :

" I had studied and restudied it so often that I knew
it backwards ; and that is about the way I sung it.   But
I must not anticipate.   The curtain rose upon the company, partly attired in evening dress; that is to say,
those who had swallow-tail coats wore them, and those
who were not blessed with that graceful garment did
the best they could.   We were arranged in the old
conventional half-circle, with the ' Goddess of Liberty '
in the centre.   The ' Mother of her Country ' had a
Roman helmet — pasteboard, I am afraid — on her
head, and was tastefully draped with the American flag.
My heart was in my mouth as the music started up,
but I stepped boldly forward to begin.   I got as far
as ' Oh, say can you see,' — and here the words left
me.   My mind was a blank.   I tried it again : ' Oh,
say, can you see — '   Whether they could see or not,
I am quite sure that I could not.   I was blind with
fright; the house swam before my eyes; the thousand
faces seemed to melt into one huge, expressionless

physiognomy.   The audience began to hiss, — oh, that
dreadful sound !   I love my country, and am, under
ordinary circumstances, fairly patriotic ; but at that

DINING-ROOM, CROW'S NEST.

moment I cursed our national anthem from the bottom of my heart. I heard the gentle voice of the Goddess of Liberty say, ' Poor fellow ! ' The remark was kind, but not encouraging. The hissing increased. Old Müller, the German leader, called out to me, ' Go on, Yo ! ' But ' Yo ' couldn't go on, so ' Yo ' thought he had better go off. I bowed, therefore, to the justice of this public rebuke, and made a graceful retreat. My poor mother stood at the wings in tears ; I threw myself into her arms, and we had it out together."

Mr. Jefferson thinks that there has been a vast improvement in public behaviour since he was hissed and jeered for so slight an offence as a momentary lapse of memory, and he attributes the improvement in manners to the free school.

Perhaps the darkest hour in young Jefferson's life occurred a few months later, when, having been stranded for several weeks in the town of Grand Gulf, Miss., and having been found by his half-brother, Charles Burke, they started for Port Gibson, where Burke's little company were to play the same evening. Burke had engaged a wagon and team to take his mother and the two children there, but when they were half-way the driver refused to go any farther until he should be paid. Burke had no money, but expected to settle the man's bill from the evening's receipts. Mrs. Jefferson's famous

Dark hours in Mississippi.

stocking had been emptied of its last coin, and there was nothing left for them but to bundle themselves unceremoniously out of the wagon and wait until Burke found some substitute. There is no little pathos in the picture that Mr. Jefferson draws of his mother, who had been "one of the most attractive stars in America, the leading prima donna of her time, reduced through no fault of her own to the humiliation of being put out of a wagon with her two children, in a lonely road in the far-off State of Mississippi, because she could not pay a wagoner the sum of ten dollars."

It was raining, and they had to wait under the shelter of a tree. But after a long time the sun came out, and soon afterwards Burke put in an appearance mounted on an ox-cart driven by an old negro. It took four hours to go the four miles to their destination, but once there, their fortunes began to mend. One night they acted in a barn, all the neighbours for miles around coming and gladly paying a dollar apiece to see a real play. Their supply of candles held out for them to give the "Lady of Lyons," but they played "The Spectre Bridegroom" by the light of the harvest moon. Mr. Winter tells a somewhat similar story, but in this case the farmer, of "more than commonly benevolent aspect," claimed all the receipts as a fair rental for his barn, and the poor actors had to walk all the way to the next town hungry

Genuine barn-storming.

and footsore. In Mr. Winter's story the distance from
the sheltering tree to Port Gibson has grown to fifteen
miles, but in either form the picture of the trials of stroll-
ing actors fifty years ago is just as vivid. They certainly
served the young Jefferson in good stead of a more for-
mal education.

After some weeks of this precarious existence, Mrs.
Jefferson was called to Galveston, and at the end of the
season there they went to Houston, where the remnant
of their company acted with just enough success to keep
"their heads above water." They were there at the
outbreak of the Mexican war, and their manager decided
to follow in the wake of the American army. They
embarked in May, 1846, for Point Isabel, where they
arrived in time to hear the firing at the battle of Palo
Alto; and the following morning Jefferson saw the
ambulance bringing in the wounded Major Ringgold.
After the capture of Matamoras, they entered the town
in the rear of the army, and obtained permission from
the commandant to occupy the old Spanish theatre,
"acting," says Jefferson, "to the most motley group
that ever filled a theatre," —soldiers, settlers, sutlers,
gamblers, and adventurers. But by the middle of
September the army had moved on to Monterey, the
town was deserted, and the manager, disbanding his
company, disappeared, leaving their salaries unpaid.

The Mexi-
can War.

Stranded in
Monterey.

The Jeffersons and one other actor, named Badger, from Philadelphia, alone were left, and being penniless, they were in desperate straits; so they called a council of war and determined to open a coffee and cake stand for the benefit of the gamblers with which the town was still swarming. There was a magnificent gambling and drinking den, called "The Grand Spanish Saloon," the proprietor of which allowed them to start their restaurant at one end, on condition that he should be paid ten per cent. of the gross receipts. Two boards placed between a dry-goods box and the counter and draped with Turkey red served as their "stand," and here "a large and elaborate tin coffee urn," heated by alcohol, and surrounded by a glittering array of cups, saucers, and German silver spoons, looked down upon their stock of pies, sandwiches, and cheap cigars. They counted much on "the large, round, burnt-sienna-looking cakes, called 'mandillos.'" These were glazed on top with some sticky substance, and served the double purpose of man-enticers and fly-traps. The stand became a great success, especially after the mandillos had been banished from sight. But a terrible murder that took place in the saloon, when three Mexicans attacked the famous Buck Wallace and stabbed him to the heart, made the young actors realise the precariousness of their calling, and they sold out.

At Matamoras Jefferson met his first love, a Spanish

Keeping a
restaurant.

girl with merry black eyes and pearly teeth. She taught
him to speak a few Spanish words, to play the guitar,
and to smoke cigarettes. At first their communications
were conducted only in the language of smiles and eyes,
and Mr. Jefferson says that it was all for the best, for
otherwise he might have astonished his mother with a
Mexican daughter-in-law. Through an interpreter he
told her that he was going back to his own country,
but that as soon as he had made his fortune he should
come back and claim her for his bride. Alas! it was
the old story of the Blue Alsatian Mountains : he never
saw her again, or any of her sixteen brothers and sisters.

A Mexican
beauty.

IV.

Return to civilisation. YOUNG Jefferson returned to New Orleans on a brig, and eagerly scanned the first newspapers to see what theatrical attractions were on hand. He went to the theatre and witnessed " King Richard III.," with Mr. and Mrs. James W. Wallack as the stars, followed by " A Kiss in the Dark," with John E. Owens as " Mr. Pittibone." It was a night to remember, for Mr. Jefferson not only conquered himself and extinguished the spark of envy that he confessed to have felt at sight of such a brilliant success, but, moreover, he felt stirred up to the great ambition and resolve to equal Owens some day.

Mrs. Jefferson and her daughter decided to remain in New Orleans, but Joseph accepted an invitation from his half-brother to join him in Philadelphia. He Performance in the stage. crossed the Alleghanies by stage-coach, and gave a travelling performance for the benefit of the passengers. He declares that he should have felt offended if they had not pressed him to do so. He sang a comic song, about " The Good Old Days of Adam and Eve," the passengers filling up the chorus. Then he indulged his auditors with what he calls " bad imi-

MANTEL, BROUGHT FROM INDIA, IN THE DINING-ROOM.

tations" of Forrest and Booth. Probably, however, his later personations on the stage were not more kindly received than these impromptu ones in the stage.

At Philadelphia, Jefferson found a warm welcome from his brother Burke, who enabled him to take parts that he now thinks were far beyond his reach, but were not beyond his ambition. He must have made considerable strides in his profession, for when Burke joined the Bowery Theatre in New York, Jefferson took his place at the Arch. One of his most amusing experiences was where Burton, the manager, revived the perennially unsuccessful "Antigone" of Sophocles (probably for the pleasure of having the audience call for the author), and Jefferson was one of the quartet that played the chorus, "done up to the chin in white Grecian togas," and crowned with laurel wreaths that continually threatened to fall off.

After acting with the stock company all winter, Mr. Jefferson took delight in going on the summer circuit as a star. It happened on the eve of one of these theatrical tramps that the people of Cumberland made the opening of their first telegraph-office a holiday, and so they crowded the theatre, and his receipts were nearly three times as much as usual, — in other words, over a hundred dollars, all in silver. As the town contained

only about five hundred inhabitants, they had to change
the bill every night, and as their finances did not at first
allow them the luxury of a bill-poster, he and his partner put up their own bills.   Mr. Jefferson says:

"No one who has not passed through the actual
experience of country management, combined with acting, can imagine the really hard work and anxiety of
it, — daily rehearsals, constant change of performance,
and the continual study of new parts ; but for all this,
there was a fascination about the life so powerful that
I have known but few that have ever abandoned it for
any other."

Glamour of
the stage.
That is true ; the public, thinking only of the successful actor, fêted, and winning great rewards, has
little realisation of the long, hard hours of work, the
dreary rehearsals, the late hours, and the perpetual
risks of failure that oppress the actor.   No wonder
that the stage-struck boy or girl, overpowered by the
glamour of the footlights, finds the reality a dreadful
awakening.

Marriage
to Margaret
Clements
Lockyer.
Mr. Jefferson, contrary to the advice of his brother,
— his mother had died in 1849, — married before he
was twenty-one.   Knowing that his friends, the other
actors, would be likely to be present at the ceremony,
" not so much out of compliment as for the purpose
of indulging in that passion for quizzing, which seems

to be so deeply planted in the histrionic breast," he boldly told the company that he was to be married at church, the following Sunday, after the morning service, and invited them to be present. The wedding took place with extreme privacy, at the Oliver Street Church, New York. His groomsman, Barney Williams, expressed his amazement, stating that he had supposed the whole company would be present. Mr. Jefferson confessed that he had sent them to the wrong church!

When Jefferson was twenty-two, he was assigned the difficult part of " Marrall," in Massinger's " New Way to Pay Old Debts," with the elder Booth in the part of " Sir Giles Overreach." Booth took much pains to *Jefferson and Booth.* teach him the business of the character, though Jefferson thinks that the great actor must have been disappointed, if not shocked, to have a stripling supporting him with so little physical or dramatic strength. But Booth's assistance and good nature were of great assistance to him. Two or three years later, he went into partnership with John Ellsler, and took a company through the South. At Macon they had good luck, but at Savannah misfortune pursued them until they happened to enlist a live baronet, the tall Sir William Don, who, though a bad actor, was intensely comical. His society connections, however, saved the season for his managers, and they ended with a blaze of glory.

The next year they repeated the experiment, sending their company on a sailing vessel from New York to Wilmington. Mr. Jefferson gives an amusing account of the vessel's departure :

A theatrical voyage.

" It was an ill-shapen hulk, with two great, badly repaired sails, flapping against her clumsy and foreboding masts. The deck and sides were besmeared with the sticky remnants of the last importation, so that when our leading actor, who had been seated on the taffrail, arose to greet his managers, he was unavoidably detained. The ladies and gentlemen of the company were uncomfortably disposed about the vessel, seated on their trunks and boxes, that had not yet been stowed away. . . . It was a doleful picture. The captain, too, was anything but a skipper to inspire confidence. He had a glazed and dishevelled look that told of last night's booze. Our second comedian, who was the reverse of being droll on the stage, but who now and then ventured a grim joke off it with better success, told me in confidence that they all had been lamenting their ill-tarred fate."

But they reached Wilmington, after a week's voyage, looking jaded and miserable. On their second evening

A balcony scene.

they gave " Romeo and Juliet," and for the balcony scene Mr. Jefferson had built up with great care a tipply construction made out of empty boxes, painted a neat

UPPER HALL, CROW'S NEST.

stone colour. The immortal love-scene was proceeding with due warmth when the quick ears of the manager heard the audience beginning to laugh; the hilarity increased. "Juliet retreated in amazement, and Romeo rushed off in despair," and when the curtain was rung hastily down Mr. Jefferson discovered to his horror that one of the boxes had been set in with the unpainted trade-mark side out, advertising a choice brand of candles.

At Charleston, S. C., they found a treasure in the beautiful Julia Dean, with whom Jefferson had acted in Mobile seven years before, and who had now risen to be the leading juvenile actress in America. So successful was her alliance that Jefferson and his partner shared $1800 for their first week's profits. With a part of this money he bought a blue enamelled watch with a diamond in the centre of the case, for his wife, and a patent lever for himself.

A successful
partnership.

The following season he was attached to the Chestnut Street Theatre, under Mr. John Gilbert, and played "Doctor Ollapod" and "Bob Acres," as well as "Doctor Pangloss." In order to represent that learned character he took his first lessons in Latin and Greek, and succeeded in pronouncing the words to the satisfaction of his audience, if not to his own. In 1853 he became stage-manager at the Baltimore Museum, and more than once went over to Washington with his company, which contained some of the best comedians of the day. Curiously enough, the "School for Scandal," produced with such an exceptional cast, was an artistic failure. Mr. Jefferson says, "Harmony is the most important element in a work of art. In this instance each piece of mosaic was perfect in form and beautiful in colour, but when fitted together they matched badly, and the effect was crude. . . . A play is like a picture : the actors are the colours, and they must blend with one another if a perfect work is to be produced."

V.

AFTER another year's experience as manager, — this time in Richmond, Va., where Agnes Robertson, Dion Boucicault, and Edwin Forrest were among his stars, — he went to Europe and had a chance to see and study many of the able comedians then acting in London.

His delight in visiting the native land of his mother's parents was unbounded. He could now add French to his other accomplishments, "getting off the French pronunciation pat and glib, as if he had lived there for years!" He also used much of the savings of two years in replenishing his theatrical wardrobe at the second-hand shops in the Temple. What a fascinating account the old actor gives of that royal expedition; of his attempts to appear cool and indifferent, of his queer misunderstandings in conversing with the little old women who had armour and robes to sell, of his solicitude lest his guide should walk off with his purchases! At one place he surprised a vivacious little flirtation between a pretty young girl, the daughter of the dealer, and two sprightly young French actors. Madame presented him to the trio as an actor from America. One of the

61

A scene
from real
life.

men, hideously ugly, with a turned-up nose and a wide gash in the middle of his face for a mouth, and the image of a monkey, assumed a grotesquely tragic air, grasped Jefferson by the hand as if he were his long-lost brother, then, pointing despairingly at the lovers, made it evident that his life was blasted by unrequited affection. Then he fell on his knees before the girl and implored her love. Her scornful laugh pricked the comedian to heart; "with a sudden spring he picked up a Roman helmet, cocked it sidewise on his head, seized a poker, and rushed upon his rival. Then he paused, and, bursting into tears, relented, and taking the lovers' hands he joined them in wedlock, invoked Heaven's blessings on them, stabbed himself with the poker, and rushed out into the front shop." It was a very gay party, but Jefferson saw plainly enough that a good deal of their fun was at his expense.

On his return to New York he joined the forces which Laura Keene had gathered for her new Broadway Theatre, and made a hit as "Doctor Pangloss," in "The Heir-at-Law." He took many liberties with the text, but in reply to a critic who charged him with "making a number of curious interpolations, occasionally using the text prepared by the author," Mr. Jefferson rightly defended his method:

"Old plays, and particularly old comedies, are filled

JOSEPH JEFFERSON IN HIS STUDIO.

with traditional introductions, good and bad. If an actor, in exercising his taste and judgment, presumes to leave out any of these respectable antiquities, he is, by the conventional critic, considered sacrilegious in ignoring them. And, on the other hand, if in amplifying the traditional business he introduces new material, he is thought to be equally impertinent; whereas the question as to the introduction should be whether it is good or bad, not whether it is old or new. If there is any preference, it should be given to the new, which must necessarily be fresh and original, while the old is only a copy." *Propriety of innovations.*

That remark well illustrates the simple common sense so characteristic of Mr. Jefferson. An actor once rated him for curtailing some of the speeches in one of the old comedies. Jefferson replied that he had his own ideas on those matters; " that the plays were written for a past age, that society had changed, and that it seemed to him good taste to alter the text, when it could be done without detriment, to suit the audience of the present day, particularly when the lines were coarse and unfit for ladies and gentlemen to speak or listen to." *Expurgated text.*

The actor insinuated that Jefferson was audacious in setting himself up as authority in such matters; that his course was a tacit reproach to older and better judges, and that " some people did that sort of thing to make professional capital out of it."

No one now will doubt that by just such scrupulous
conduct as that, Jefferson has done his great share in
elevating the tone and morale of the stage, and it never
really injured him either with the public or with the profession that on account of it he was for a time called " the
Sunday-school Comedian."

His dictum that a man has no more right to be offen-
sive on the stage than in the drawing-room might well be
the motto of every theatre.

The panic
of 1857.

During the panic of 1857, Mr. Jefferson tried his
hand at concocting a melodrama from a Revolutionary
story entitled " Blanche of Brandywine."   It was so full
of " battles, marches, countermarches, murders, abduc-
tions, hairbreadth escapes, militia trainings and extravagant Yankee comicalities," that it made audiences forget
their anxieties caused by falling stocks and failing banks.
It has been said that during panics theatres are gen-
erally well patronised, but at this time, Mr. Jefferson
says, "the public despondently stayed at home, the
theatres were empty, the managers depressed."   But
he notes that the actors were always in the best of
spirits when business was bad and salaries were un-
certain.

VI.

THE year 1858 brought great good fortune to Joseph "Asa Trenchard." Jefferson. Tom Taylor's comedy, "The American Cousin," was presented for the first time. It had been offered to several experienced managers, who rejected it, and it was reserved for an inexperienced business-manager to discover its latent possibilities. It was recommended to Jefferson, who was greatly taken with the naturalness of the love-scenes and instantly saw the chance of making something out of the leading part.

It made the fortune of three of the actors. At the rehearsal, and indeed for the first fortnight, E. H. Sothern found everything to depress him in the part of " Lord Dundreary," but as he began to add all sorts of extravagances to his acting, the originality of the character began to dawn on him, until he made it a personation of world-wide fame. Jefferson, as "Asa Trenchard," took his place instantly as one of America's leading actors. Mr. Winter says :

"Seldom has an actor found a medium for the expression of his spirit so ample and so congenial as that part proved for Jefferson. Rustic grace, simple manliness,

67

unconscious drollery, and unaffected pathos, expressed with artistic control, and in an atmosphere of repose, could not have been more truthfully and beautifully combined."

The play ran for the whole season, — one hundred and forty nights,—and in the summer, having parted from Laura Keene's company, Jefferson took it through the " provinces."

"Caleb Plummer."

His next great success was as "Caleb Plummer" in an adaptation of Dickens's "Cricket on the Hearth," which was played at Boucicault's "Winter Garden." After the first night Boucicault said to him: "If that is the way you intend to act the part, I don't wonder you were afraid to undertake it." Jefferson, who had expressed his fear that he could not act a part requiring

Boucicault drops a valuable hint.

pathos, was nevertheless willing to learn, so he asked the experienced actor what he meant. The reply was: "You have acted your last scene first; if you begin in that solemn strain, you have nothing left for the end of the play."

Jefferson declares that the common sense underlying this remark so appealed to him that he acted upon it, and so achieved success. He learned not to anticipate strong effects, but to lead the audience up to a proper climax. He succeeded in raising the part to such a degree of perfection that the critics said of him, " The

LANDSCAPE BY JEFFERSON, '96 (PAINTING).

gentle old man of Dickens's story lives again in him and touches every heart by his sweet self-sacrifice. Jefferson's sensibility makes him sympathetic with the character, while his admirable art enables him to embody it with thorough precision of detail."

He was also successful in the parts of " Newman Noggs," " Salem Scudder," " Granby Gag," and others, and when Boucicault suddenly withdrew, Jefferson's version of " Oliver Twist " was presented with immense success with J. W. Wallack as " Fagin " and Matilda Heron as " Nancy." He was not so successful in the humorous portraiture in Mrs. Bateman's version of " Evangeline." He declared it was the worst comic part he had ever played.

VII

THE actor who has had success in a part, the actor who has written a play, cannot fail to keep his eyes open for further possibilities ; his ambition will be stimulated to create some character that shall be his, and his alone. Jefferson says that when the curtain descended on the first night of " The American Cousin," he then and there resolved to be " a star." He had made his audience both laugh and cry. That great marriage of dramatic powers, the Humorous and the Pathetic, is the source of all success.

One rainy day in the summer of 1859, while he was reading the " Life and Letters of Washington Irving," in the hayloft of a barn in Paradise Valley, at the foot of Pocono Mountain, in Pennsylvania, he happened to come across his own name in a passage where Irving had noted that the younger Jefferson was like his father in " look, gesture, size, and make." He had never seen Jefferson's father, and of course meant his grandfather. By a natural transition he was led to think of " Rip Van Winkle." An American story by an American author for an American actor ! He hastened into the house

and got "The Sketch-Book," but on re-reading the
story of " Rip," he was disappointed to find it so un-
dramatic. In Irving's placid narrative it is merely the
old story of the Cretan poet Epimenides (whom St. Paul
quotes in Titus), believed by the ancients to have been
sent out by his father after the sheep and to have fallen
fast asleep (like the likewise mythical little Bo-Peep),
only to awaken at the end of fifty-seven years, and find
the whole world changed.

Within nine years after the publication of "The Dramatisa-
tions of
" Rip Van
Winkle."
Sketch-Book," Thomas Flynn had made a poor dramati-
sation of " Rip," and several others had followed. In
1829, Jefferson's aunt Elizabeth had played in one,
supposed to have been a version made in England.
Charles Burke made still another in 1849, and Jefferson
acted the part of the innkeeper, Seth. There were no
less than seven predecessors to Jefferson in the part of An ideal
play.
" Rip Van Winkle." Mr. Winter, who gives an inter-
esting account of the various versions, says :

" All the salient extremes of a representative picture
of human experience are found in it, — fact and fancy;
youth and age ; love and hatred ; loss and gain ; mirth
and sadness ; humour and pathos ; rosy childhood and
decrepit senility ; lovers with their troubles, which will
all be smoothed away, and married people with their
anxieties, which will never cease ; life within doors, and

life among trees and mountains; the domestic and the
romantic; the natural and the preternatural; and through
all, the development and exposition of a humorous, cheer-
ing, romantic, restful human character. Such a theme
cannot be too much commended to thoughtful consideration. It is prolific of lessons for the conduct of life.
It teaches no direct moral; but its power is in its influ-
ence, — to lure us away from absorption in the busy
world, and to make us hear again the music of running
water and rippling leaves, the wind in the pine-trees, the
surf upon the beach, and, under all, the distant murmur
of that great ocean to which our spirits turn, and into
which we must vanish."

Some persons would go even further than Mr. Winter, and argue that in Mr. Jefferson's presentation of the
henpecked tippler he taught a lesson in temperance
more powerful than any temperance lecture ever de-
livered.

A new way
of preparing
for a play.

Mr. Jefferson remembered several of the versions of
the story, but none of them seemed to give him what he
wanted. He went down to the city and got together
"Rip's" wardrobe before he had written a line of the
play. He does not recommend this way as the ideal
method of writing a play, but tells the story to illustrate
the impatience and enthusiasm with which he entered on
his task. He got the three printed versions of the play,

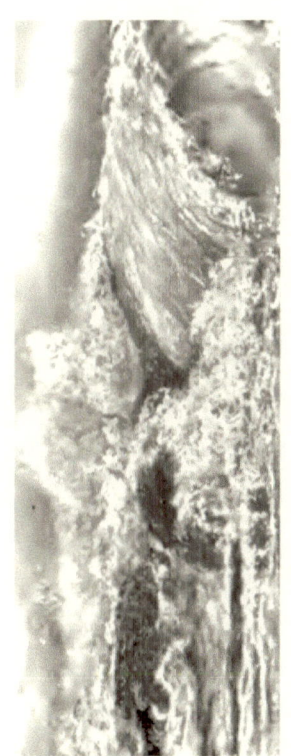

and compared them. They were in two acts, and in all of them the spectre crew was introduced as speaking and singing. Jefferson divided the play into three acts, and made the second act wholly a monologue, while Sir Hendrik Hudson's companions merely gesticulate. Though it took considerable thought to arrange the questions so that the answers might be made by ghostly nods, yet, within a few days, he had his version of the play all ready, and he learned and rehearsed the part, so that in the early fall he was enabled to present it to the public in Washington. It won sufficient success to prove to him that the character was what he was after; nevertheless, the play was not satisfactory. "The action," he says, "had neither the body nor the strength to carry the hero; the spiritual quality was there, but the human interest was wanting."

Early
defects of
" Rip Van
Winkle."

VIII.

In 1861, Mrs. Jefferson died, and the New York
home was broken up. Leaving three of his children
at school, he started with his eldest son for California.
He states that his engagement in San Francisco was an
unmistakable failure, and he attributes the cause of it
to the overzeal of his manager, who had raised expecta-
tions too high, or, in theatrical parlance, had "overbilled"
him. However that may have been, he acted there, ac-
according to Mr. Winter, for nearly four months. In
September,— Mr. Winter says November,— he sailed
for Australia in the clipper-ship *Nimrod*. On board
ship he had great success as a theologian, and his
arguments were so powerful in favour of marriage, that
his fellow-passenger, Father O'Grady, had not been in
Sydney three years before he renounced his orders,
and married, though he still remained faithful to his
church. Mr. Jefferson came to the conclusion that
it was the beauty of the lady, rather than his good
advice, that had overcome the "good St. Anthony's"
scruples.

In Australia, Mr. Jefferson depended for his support

on talent there assembled, and as he brought a number of fresh plays, such as "Rip Van Winkle," "Our American Cousin," and "The Octoroon," he made a great sensation. At Melbourne his engagement reached one hundred and sixty-four consecutive nights. At Castlemaine, he was introduced to the notice of the inhabitants by a town crier, who, dressed in a high white hat and seedy black suit, stood on a barrel in front of the theatre, crying:

"Oh, yes! Oh, yes! Oh, yes! Step up, ladies and gentlemen; now or never is your honly chance to see the greatest living wonder of the age, Joseph Jefferson, the great hactor from Amerikee. His power of producing tears at vun and the same time is so great that he caused the Emperor of Roushia to weep on his weddin' night, and made her gracious Majesty, the Queen, bu'st out laughin' at the funeral of Prince Albert. He is the bosom friend of the President of Amerikee, and the hidol of 'is Royal 'Ighness, the Prince of Wales." *A town crier.*

That was too much for the modest and truth-loving Jefferson, and he declared that he would not act unless the little bell-man should be suppressed. This was more of a job than the manager had expected. Mr. Jefferson describes the scene with that delightful humour which always enlivens his conversation:

A comic
scene.

"The little fat man now stood with his arms folded, glaring defiance at the manager and his myrmidons, but they seized him, and a tremendous struggle ensued. The tall white hat was completely mashed over his eyes, and in stamping violently with his rage, the head of the barrel burst in, letting him through, till only a fat head just appeared above the top. They tipped the barrel over, and rolled him off inside, to the great amusement of the bystanders, who had been roaring with laughter all the time."

Mr. Jefferson not only toured through the various large cities of Australia, but visited the interior, and saw a good deal of interesting life among the natives; but he confesses that he never learned to throw a boom-

Kean and
the
boomerang.

erang with native skill. He gives an interesting picture of himself, sitting with the great English actor, Edmund Kean, on a bench in St. Kilda Park, watching a party of blacks throwing the boomerang.

A convict
play played
to convicts.

In Hobart Town, the capital of Van Diemen's Land, Mr. Jefferson played "The Ticket-of-Leave Man" for the first time. The city had a large element of former convicts, and the announcement of the play aroused great excitement among the Tasmaniacs (as H. J. Byron called them). Mr. Winter says that upwards of six hundred ticket-of-leave men were included in his audience on one occasion. Mr. Jefferson says:

THE MILL, BY JEFFERSON, '97 (PAINTING).

"At least one hundred ticket-of-leave men were in the pit on the first night of its production." Before the curtain rose, he looked out, and thought it the most terrible audience he had ever seen. "Men with low foreheads, and small, peering, ferret-looking eyes; some with flat noses, and square, cruel jaws; some with sinister expression, leering, low and cunning, all wearing a sullen, dogged look, as if they would tear the benches from the pit and gut the theatre of its scenery if one of their kind was held up to public scorn upon the stage."

The impersonation of "Bob Brierly" was an immense success; the audience rose to him and "cheered to the very echo." Jefferson was more than once accosted in the street by less innocent congeners of poor "Bob," who would tell him some touching story of their early days.

He also visited New Zealand, where the old comedies proved most successful, and then, after a short return engagement in Australia, he sailed from Melbourne in a clipper-ship for South America. It had taken him fifty-seven days from San Francisco to Melbourne; it took fifty-seven days for him to reach Callao. On the first voyage the only excitement was religious discussions with Father O'Grady; on this voyage a Northern man and a Southerner were among the passengers, and Mr. Jefferson had to act as peacemaker, so belligerent were their

Jefferson as peacemaker.

discussions of politics.   It was during the sixties, and the
result of the war of the Rebellion had not yet been

At Callao. announced.   A Callao ship-calker, formerly from the
States, recognised Mr. Jefferson as soon as he set eyes
on him ; he brought them the tidings, "The war's over:
the South caved in and Richmond is took."

This same theatrical connoisseur offered to enable Jefferson to see the "Spanish fandango" danced, but as
the place was rather dangerous, he declined.   He was
amazed at the beauty of the ladies of Lima, at the horse-
back-riding beggars, and at the religious fervour and the
religious democracy of all classes, as they mingled in
the dingy cathedral.

He was kept a week in Peru before the ship sailed for
Panama, and it was not until June, 1865, that he reached

The new
"Rip Van
Winkle." London.   There he met Dion Boucicault, who, without
much enthusiasm for the subject, agreed to rewrite Jefferson's "Rip Van Winkle" for a consideration.   Mr.
Clarke Davis says that many of the suggested changes
came from Jefferson ; the impressive ending of the first
act was Boucicault's, while the climax of the third act —
Menie recognising her father — is merely the reverse of
King Lear recognising Cordelia.   Boucicault also introduced the scheme of the second marriage and many of
the now familiar details.   Boucicault told Jefferson that
it could not possibly keep the stage more than a month,

but Billington, one of the London cast, told Paul Bedford, the original "Nick Vedder," "There's a hundred nights in that play."

A quarrel between Boucicault and Webster, the manager of the Adelphi Theatre, nearly resulted in the play being withdrawn before it was presented, but Mr. Jefferson's tact prevented this calamity, and the fateful night approached. Mr. Jefferson gives an amusing description of his last private rehearsal. It was Sunday evening, and he was alone in his lodging, and had got out his new wig and beard for the last scene. He put them on and began acting and posing in front of the mirror.

In about twenty minutes there came a knock at the door. This dialogue ensued:

"Who's there?"

"It's me," said the gentle but agitated voice of the chambermaid. "May I come in?"

A public rehearsal.

"Certainly not," replied Mr. Jefferson, for he had no desire to be seen in his disguise.

"Is there anything wrong in the room, sir?" she asked.

"Nothing at all. Go away."

"Well, sir, there's a policeman at the door, and he says as 'ow there's a crazy old man in your room, a flingin' of 'is 'ands and a-goin' on hawful, and there's a crowd of people across the street a-blockin' hup the way."

Mr. Jefferson turned to the window and discovered to his horror that he had forgotten to draw down the curtain. At first he was mortified at having thus unconsciously acted before an audience of deadheads, but afterwards the comicality of the situation so overcame him that he laughed till he was cured of a sharp attack of indigestion.

The London critics hailed Jefferson as one of the most genuine artists that had ever appeared on the British stage, and large audiences made his engagement a triumphant success.

At New York again. After playing a farewell engagement in Manchester and Liverpool, he took a sailing vessel for New York, and on the third of September, 1866, appeared at the Olympic Theatre, where his performance of "Rip" won immense applause. As Mr. Winter says, "The fame of its beauty soon ran over the land." He also revived "The American Cousin" and other old comedies, in each winning the heartiest commendation. At the close of that management he went West, and in December, 1867, was married in Chicago to his second wife, Miss Sarah Isabel Warren, the niece of William Warren, his father's cousin. He now used some of his savings in buying homes. In 1869 he purchased an estate near Yonkers, another at Hohokus, N. J., on the Saddle River, and a third, consisting of a ruined plantation on a lovely island

in Louisiana. His relative, John B. Rice, of Chicago, rated him for his extravagance in buying " a large planta- tion in the South, with nothing left of the sugar-house but the chimney, all the fences and everything in a di- lapidated condition," and calling it an investment ! Jef- ferson suggested that in time the orange groves might pay him ; but when, some years afterwards, his son in- formed him that the only profits on a large consignment of oranges, after deducting the expenses, were three two- cent postage-stamps, he concluded that " Uncle John " was about right.

Profitable Investment.

The plantation is situated on an island of about two hundred acres, high above the sea, and covered with splendid live-oak and magnolia trees, as well as with the oranges and pecans that were in bloom when he bought it. Formerly a famous buccaneer had made the island his haunt, and the natives of the region imagine that there are hoards of precious treasures buried along its shores or under the trees. The gold and silver that is hidden by pirates during the last century on our seaboard would pay off the national debt. From New- foundland to Ogunquit, and from Cape Cod to the Mississippi, the whole coast, if one may judge by the mounds that one sees near Bald Head Cliff, must have been dug up a score of times,—at night, too, with weird incantations. No wonder that Mr. Jefferson objects to

Pirates' hoards.

the disfiguring of the picturesque shores of the Bayou
Têche. His description of their arrival at his Southern
home is a picture in words; it must not be forgotten
that Mr. Jefferson is a painter of pictures as well as an
actor :

"At Brashear, the terminus of the railway, we used to
get on board of a little stern-wheel boat, so small that,
contrasted with the leviathan Texas steamers anchored
in the bay, it looked like a toy. Our route lay west-
ward, up the Bayou Atchafalaya to where it met the
Bayou Têche. This is the point where Gabriel and
Evangeline are separated in Longfellow's poem. Our
passage up the Têche was extremely picturesque. The
stream is narrow, and the live-oak and cypress trees
stretch their branches over it till in places they fairly
meet and interlock. When the darkness came on, pine-
knots were burned in the bow of the boat, and as she
steamed up the narrow river a strong light fell on the
gaunt trees that suddenly started out of the black night
like weird spectres. The negro deck-hands, some bare
to the waist, and others in red and blue shirts, would
sit in lazy groups chanting their plantation songs, keeping perfect time with the beat of the engine."

And the pleasure of the arrival at this paradise of
leisure, where, amid a kindly population, the kind-
hearted owners would enter into their season of rest!

A picture
in words.

Mr. Jefferson reports one amusing conversation with A showman's duties. a coloured boy, who had paddled him out duck-hunting on the bayou. This was the dialogue:

" Mr. Joe, will you be mad if I ax you somefen?"

" No, John; what is it?"

" What does you do in a show?"

" That is rather hard to explain."

" Well, does you swallow knives?"

" No; I have no talent that way."

" Why, your son tole me that you swallowed knives and forks and fire and de Lawd knows what all; I b'lieve he was jest a-foolin' of me."

" He's quite capable of it."

" Well, dere's one thing certain; you don't act in the circus."

" How can you be sure of that?"

" Oh, no sah,— oh, no sah; you cain't fool me on dat. I've seen you get on your horse; you ain't no circus rider."

By taking long vacations in this enchanting Southern home, by making his seasons comparatively short, and Short Seasons. by reserving several off-nights each week, Mr. Jefferson diminished the monotony of acting his great part. And when he once more came back to the boards, he was as fresh as at the very beginning. He played it for the first time in Boston in the summer of 1869, and shortly

after Booth's splendid theatre was opened he began a
triumphant series of seasons there. It has been esti-
mated that upwards of 150,000 persons witnessed his
Rip at that one theatre.

The little
church
around the
corner.
In 1870, the veteran actor, George Holland, died, and
Mrs. Holland's sister desired the funeral to be held at
her own church. Mr. Jefferson, as an old friend of the
family, went to the minister with one of Holland's sons.
Mr. Jefferson told the rector that his friend was an actor,
and the rector replied that in the circumstances he should
have to decline holding the services at the church. The
boy was in tears at such a reply. Mr. Jefferson was too
indignant to say a word, but as they left the room he
paused and asked if there was any other church from
which his friend might be buried. The rector replied
that there was a little church around the corner where it
might be done. Mr. Jefferson said, "Then if this be
so, God bless 'the little church around the corner.'"
From that time forth the Rev. Mr. ———'s church
bore that famous appellation. In the following January
Mr. Jefferson played the part of " Mr. Golightly," in the
amusing farce of " Lend me Five Shillings," given, with
other plays, for the benefit of George Holland's widow
and children. His personation of that fascinating and
laughable character was regarded as one of his most
brilliant successes.

JEFFERSON'S STABLE, SHOWING HIS YOUNGEST SON ON PONY.

When Mr. Jefferson was about forty-three, he was attacked by glaucoma and threatened with complete blindness. The oculist assured him that unless he submitted to an immediate operation his case would be hopeless. It was performed at his home at Hohokus and proved entirely successful. In August he was enabled to write to a friend, " All traces of the disease have entirely disappeared. I no longer wear glasses, and in fact am as good as new." *Threatened blindness.*

By the following January he reappeared on the stage with greater popularity than ever. And he soon transferred his conquests to England. The summer before his season opened in London he spent with his family in Paris. He gives an amusing account of his attempts to learn French, — " the pure, solid mother tongue, with a full Parisian accent." He pictures his celebrated teacher, who came dressed in the extreme of tawdry fashion, full of flounces and frills, with a large head decked out in an enormous bonnet and smothered in a flower-garden in full bloom, hugging three or four big books under one arm, and flourishing a formidable blue cotton umbrella. His progress was so rapid that, he says, at the end of the first month, by hard study and close application, he knew less about it than when he began. So he abdicated in favour of his children, and spent the happy days painting pictures of old châteaux or picturesque cottages embowered under *Learning French and painting pictures.*

tall poplar trees.   It was during this visit that Mr. Jefferson gathered together some of the beautiful specimens of French art that were later destroyed when his summer cottage was burnt down.   His criticism on the French school is very interesting.   He says:

Art
criticism.
" I am of the opinion that the greatest landscapes are works of the imagination rather than transcripts of realities.   Nature refuses to be imitated, but invariably rewards the artist who has the modesty to suggest her.   The painter who attempts to give an exact picture of a natural scene will find himself surrounded by insurmountable difficulties.   As an example, let us suppose that he takes for his subject a certain view with which we are familiar; the sky, water, foreground, trees, and distance may be painted in the exact form, colour, and perspective proportions of the original, and yet fail to give one idea of the spot.   What is the reason of this non-resemblance when all the details have been so carefully imitated?   What is it that has no existence in the picture, and that so pervades nature?   Where are the sweet sounds of the woods?   Where is the singing of the birds, the hum of busy insects, and the murmur of the brooks ?   Where is the movement of the clouds, the graceful bending of the trees, and the perfume of the pines and woodland flowers?   He cannot paint these, and so his realistic work is cold and lifeless.   But if in modest truth he suggests his work, omitting hard

details and impertinent finish, the simple picture will lead us in our imagination to supply the artistic impossibilities of sound and movement."

These suggestions are extremely interesting, for Mr. Jefferson has won no small success in the art of landscape painting, and some of his pictures well illustrate this very quality of which he speaks.

IX.

MR. JEFFERSON spent two winters in London at the Princess's Theatre, and ended his London engagement with a brief season at which he played "Mr. Golightly" and other light comedy parts. His London life was made memorable by his friendship or acquaintance with some of the greatest men of the day. He was invited to make a visit at a splendid estate in Scotland, and there he had a

A retort courteous.

memorable encounter with the daughter of an English earl. She was radiantly beautiful, "witty, aristocratic, haughty, and satirical," and she amused herself by quizzing the American actor. At first he took her questions seriously, but soon perceived that she was making sport of him, and when she asked him with apparent innocence if he had lately met the Queen, he replied with equal seriousness, "No, madam, I was out when her Majesty called." He was revenged.

Before he came back to America he played "Rip" in Dublin and Belfast. In the one the engagement was a flat failure; indeed, he was asked at the first rehearsal to make the character Irish instead of Dutch, and he was told that if he would do so the Dublin audience was such

a rare one that he might **defy** the world.   **He** declares
that if the scarcity **of spectators was a test of its** rareness,
it certainly was.

After his return to America he confined himself **prin-**   Versatility.
cipally to his two great parts.   **Assuredly, he who had**
won **his laurels in over a** hundred distinct characters did
not deserve the reproach **of lacking** versatility.   In ref-
erence to this charge, — that **he has** been remiss in **learning new** parts, — he quotes a conversation with Charles
Mathews, in which that clever comedian rallied him as
" the prince of dramatic carpetbaggers," **carrying** all his
wardrobe **in a gripsack.   But Mr.** Jefferson retorted
that he was confounding wardrobe with talent, and assured him that "it requires more skill to act one part
fifty different ways, than to act fifty parts all one way."

For his own sake an actor needs some **change, and
Mr. Jefferson, who** had come upon " Rip **Van** Winkle "
after long search, found the part of " Bob Acres " obsess-
ing him in somewhat the same **way as " Rip "** had done.
He says : " Bob **was an attractive fellow** to contemplate.   " Bob Acres " an ideal part.
Sheridan had filled him with such quaintness and eccen-
tricity that he became to me irresistible.   I would often
think of him in the middle of the night.   At odd times,
when there was apparently no reason for him to call, he
would pop up before me like a new acquaintance, — for
I had acted him before, — but always with a new expres-

sion on his face. The variety of situations in which the author had placed him ; his arrival in town with his shallow head full of nonsense and curl-papers, and his warm heart overflowing with love for an heiress who could not endure him in the country because he used to dress so badly ; a nature soft and vain, with a strong mixture of goose and peacock ; his aping of the fashion of the town, with an unmistakable survival of rural manners ; his swagger and braggadocio while writing a challenge ; and, above all, the abject fright that falls upon him when he realises what he has done, — could the exacting heart of a comedian ask for more than these?"

So he fell to work, condensing and revising, and, in fact, largely rewriting "The Rivals," just as Sheridan himself had altered and renamed Vanbrugh's comedy of "The Relapse." He condensed the play from five acts to three, he cut several of the characters out of it, and he expunged the few lines that had any shadow of coarseness about them.

Innovations. At the first rehearsal at Philadelphia, Mrs. John Drew introduced some novel business in the part of "Mrs. Malaprop," and asked him if he thought the innovation was admissible. Mr. Jefferson replied that he thought it was ; moreover, that he was convinced that Sheridan himself would have done the same thing, if he had only thought of it. The revised play was warmly received,

ELECTRIC PLANT.

but of course some of the old actors felt called upon to indulge in harmless sarcasms. Jefferson's cousin, William Warren, remarked that it reminded him of Thomas Buchanan Read's poem, "And Sheridan twenty miles away." John Gilbert predicted that the shade of Sheridan would haunt him. At a Christmas tree, when his manager received a bundle of railway guides, his gift was a book of "The Rivals," with all the parts but his own cut out. But all this was innocent fun. Mr. Winter, in a long and careful analysis of the part, says, "The spirit of Jefferson's impersonation was humanity and sweet good nature, while the traits that he especially emphasised were ludicrous vanity and comic trepidation. He left no moment unfilled with action, when he was on the scene, and all his by-play was made tributary to the expression of these traits."

Since 1880, then, Mr. Jefferson's life has been one which any actor might set for himself as an ideal. Limiting himself to a repertoire of not more than a dozen characters, and for the greater part of the time to only two, — "Rip" and "Bob Acres," — he has made short seasons, and played to full and profitable houses. Age has not dimmed the fervour of those immortal impersonations. During the hard months of winter he has sought, and apparently found, Ponce de Leon's fountain of eternal youth on his beautiful estate of Orange Island.

A delightful old age.

Here is the picture of him, painted by himself, in his
serene old age:

"In Louisiana the live-oak is the king of the forest,
and the magnolia is its queen; and there is nothing more
delightful than to sit under them on a clear, calm spring
morning like this. The old limbs twine themselves in
fantastic forms, the rich, yellow foliage mantles the trees
with a sheen of gold, and from beneath the leaves, the
gray moss is draped, hanging in graceful festoons, and
swaying slowly in the gentle air. I am listening to the
merry chirp of the tuneful cardinal, as he sparkles like a
ruby amid the green boughs, and to the more glorious
melody of the mocking-bird. Now, in the distance,
comes the solemn cawing of two crafty crows; they are
far apart; one sits on the high branch of a dead cypress,
while his cautious mate is hidden away in some secluded
spot; they jabber to each other as though they held a
conference of deep importance; he on the high limb
gives a croak as though he made a signal to his distant
mate, and here she comes out of the dense wood and
lights quite near him on the cypress branch; they sidle
up to each other, and lay their wise old heads together,
now seeming to agree upon a plan of action; with one
accord they flutter from the limb, and slowly flap themselves away.

"I am sitting here upon the fragment of a broken

A picture in
words.

wheel; the wood is fast decaying, and the iron cogs are rusting in their age. It is as old as I am, but will last much longer. Most likely it belonged to some old mill, and has been here in idleness, through generations of the crows; it must have done good service in its day, and if it were a sentient wheel, perhaps would feel the comfort, in old age, of having done its duty.

"Over my head the gray arms of two live-oaks stretch their limbs, and looking down into the ravine, I see the trees are arched, as though they canopied the aisle of a cathedral; and doubtless they stood here before the builder of the mill was born. Behind a fallen tree there stands another; and on the trunk, from where I sit, I plainly see the initials of my wife's name, cut there by me on some romantic birthday, many years ago."

We can see Mr. Jefferson surrounded by members of his family in this Southern paradise; his genial, shrewd, expressive face beaming with happy thoughts. One can fill in the figure painting in addition to his own landscape.

When the summer breezes blow too torrid across the waters of the bayou, Mr. Jefferson flits like the birds to the North. He has a charming estate called Crow's Nest, near the upper waters of Buzzard's Bay. The

Crow's Nest.

house which was built in 1889 was filled with many
choice works of art, — a portrait of Mrs. Siddons, by
Sir Joshua Reynolds, a portrait of himself by Wilkie,
and other pictures by Lawrence, Corot, Daubigny, Tro-
yon, Rousseau, Diaz, and others. By the explosion of
a gasolene tank, Crow's Nest was set on fire, and burnt
to the ground, with all its precious contents, in April,
1893. The following year it was rebuilt, and here, in
summer, Mr. Jefferson lives a delightful life, in intimate association with ex-President Cleveland and other
congenial friends. Buzzard's Bay offers every enticing
sport, with its bluefish, and a safe expanse for boating.
Not far away are the charming ponds of the Cape,
where trout and bass abound. The scenery is not

The
beauties of
Buzzard's
Bay.

magnificent, but the quiet landscape is full of charm;
in driving over the hard shell roads that cut across
the sandy soil, there are fascinating glimpses of blue
water, and there are wild tracts, where not a house can
be seen. The air is peculiarly soft and balmy, and
the daily breeze from the Bay tempers the extreme
heat of the equinox.

Here Mr. Jefferson gathers around him, not only his
own children, — of which ten have been born to him, —
but also his children's children; and any one who has
ever seen Rip with the children of Falling Water will
not hesitate to believe that Mr. Jefferson is fond of

children, and some of the most attractive portraits of him show him with children at his knee or climbing over his back.

He still paints enthusiastically, and some of his pictures have been shown in exhibitions, always attracting great interest, not merely because they are the work of the popular actor, but because they have intrinsic merit. Their dominant quality has been described as being akin to his acting: " marked by tenderness of feeling, combined with a touch of mystery," — an imaginative quality, reminding of the works of Corot. It is no small privilege to be admitted to the sanctum of Mr. Jefferson's studio, where he so skilfully wields the brush and mahlstick. It is certainly an instructive sight to see a man who has won fame and fortune in a calling that tends to unsettle domesticity, thus utilising his pleasant leisure with an avocation so ennobling and satisfactory. *Mr. Jefferson as an artist.*

His residence in Louisiana is so far away, and in so large a domain, — Mr. Winter calls it six hundred acres, — that he seems to disappear from sight when he gets there. But at Buzzard's Bay he is in the eye of the world. His noble mansion stands out prominent on a breezy height, overlooking the Bay; and here he may be seen with his family, or entertaining the guests who delight in his genial hospitality and ever-fluent store of anecdote, reminiscence, and wit. *Genial hospitality.*

The house itself is filled with valuable relics, with art treasures brought from all parts of the world.   His own

Art works
at Crow's
Nest.

pictures hang upon the walls, and hold their own in comparison with those of men who have made painting their life-work, rather than a diversion.   The mantelpiece in the dining-room was brought from India, is richly carved, and is in itself a work of art.   Under the mantel in the parlor is a panel representing, in relief, scenes from "Rip Van Winkle."   The electrical lighting is furnished from a power-house situated on the premises, and, typical of its owner, keeps the whole establishment in a glow of brilliancy.   Ample stables furnish recreation in riding and driving.   In fact, Crow's Nest is a home, — a home of wealth and comfort and cosiness.

Four of Mr. Jefferson's sons have either adopted the stage, or shown talent for the drama.   One of his daughters is married to the distinguished English novelist, Benjamin L. Farjeon, author of "The King of Noland" and "Miriam Rozella."   She lives in London.   His youngest son was born in 1885.

X.

ONE might fill many pages with analyses of Mr. Jefferson will be remembered. Jefferson's impersonations. They have been so many times described that it will not be hard for those of another generation to get some idea of his powers. Yet even the present generation will remember him chiefly as the creator of "Rip Van Winkle" and "Bob Acres." These two parts, so dissimilar and yet with somewhat the same strength and the same lovable weaknesses, have amused and delighted unnumbered thousands. Mr. Jefferson's success in working out an original conception for these parts teaches a lesson to persons of every age and every profession; it is to have an ideal, and constantly to strive to reach it. To be sure, Mr. Jefferson seems to have inherited peculiar talent for the profession into which he was born, and circumstances favoured his training in it in a school not by any means easy, but nevertheless adequate to bring out his best qualities. Throughout his course, he shaped every change and possibility so as to bear on his coming mastership. It was, therefore, something better than "Good Fortune" that brought him such an immense

measure of reward.   No one can grudge him the good
An amiable
character. things that have fallen to his share.   He has preserved
in all circumstances the sweet and wholesome sense that
acts as a salt against conceit.   His friends are unanimous
in their praise of his simplicity, cordiality, and frankness.
To have reached to the serene old age of fourscore "so
unspotted of the world," is as fine a lesson of genius as
history can afford.

THE END.

www.ingramcontent.com/pod-product-compliance
Lightning Source LLC
Chambersburg PA
CBHW032148010726
47493CB00008BA/2634